World of Reading

STAR WARS™

CAPTURED ON CLOUD CITY

WRITTEN BY NATE MILLICI

ART BY PILOT STUDIO

PRESS
Los Angeles • New York

S0-DVC-756

© & TM 2017 Lucasfilm Ltd.

All rights reserved. Published by Disney • Lucasfilm Press, an imprint of Buena Vista Books, Inc. No part of this book may be reproduced or transmitted in any form or by any means, electronic or mechanical, including photocopying, recording, or by any information storage and retrieval system, without written permission from the publisher. For information address Disney • Lucasfilm Press, 1200 Grand Central Avenue, Glendale, California 91201.

Printed in China

First Boxed Set Edition, July 2017 10 9 8 7 6

Library of Congress Control Number on file

FAC-025393-21207

ISBN 978-1-368-01493-9

Visit the official *Star Wars* website at: www.starwars.com.

The *Millennium Falcon* raced toward
the floating Cloud City above Bespin.
The ship had escaped
from the Empire.
But it was badly damaged.

Han, Leia, Chewie, and C-3PO
needed help!
Han's old friend Lando
invited them to stay with him.
Lando said he would
help fix the *Falcon*.

But the team was still in danger!
First C-3PO wandered away
and was hit by blaster fire.

Then Darth Vader arrived!
Han fired his blaster.
But Darth Vader used the Force
to deflect Han's blasts.

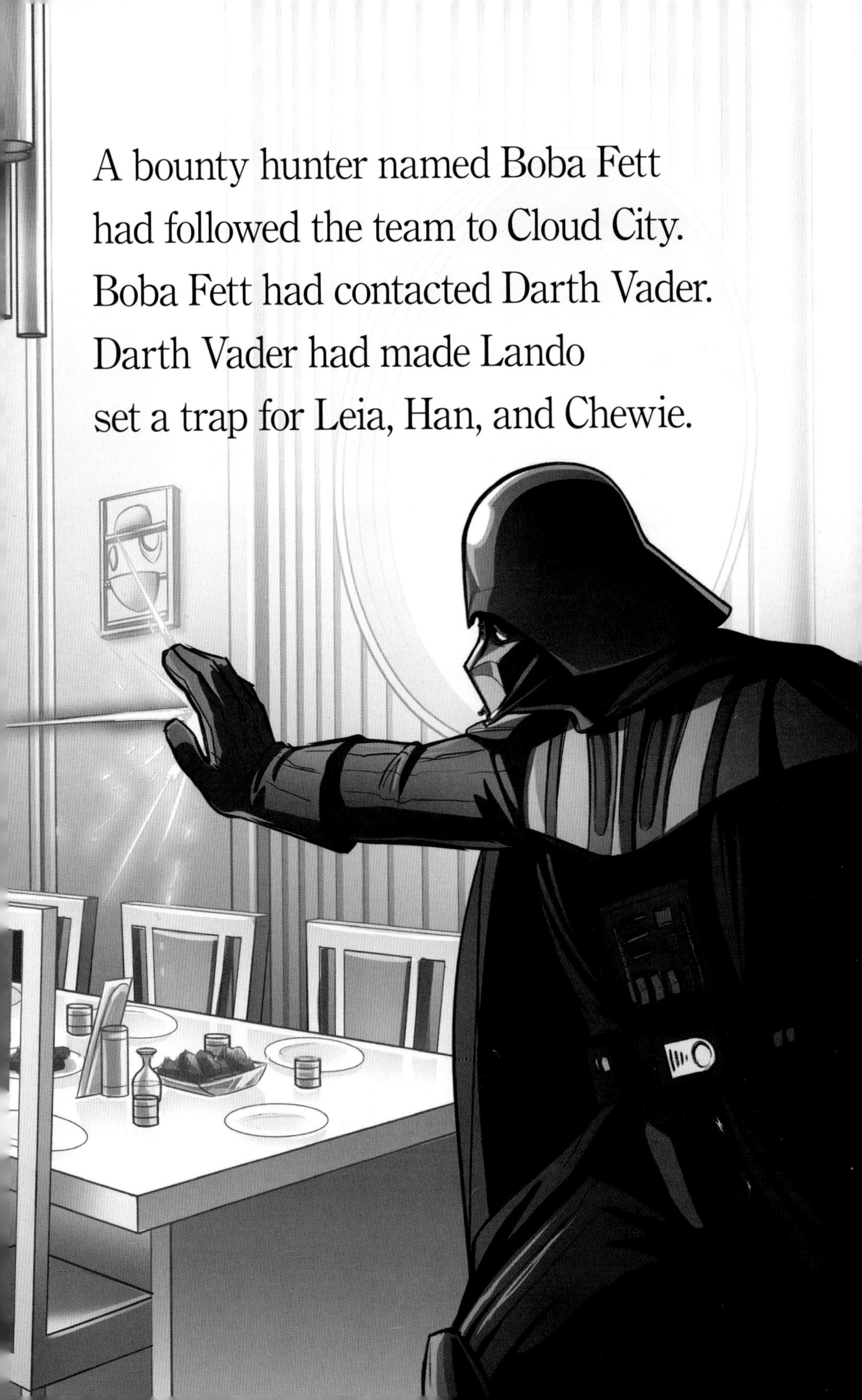

A bounty hunter named Boba Fett
had followed the team to Cloud City.
Boba Fett had contacted Darth Vader.
Darth Vader had made Lando
set a trap for Leia, Han, and Chewie.

Darth Vader locked up
Leia, Han, and Chewie.
Leia and Han did not
know what to do.
Chewie tried to put
C-3PO back together.

Darth Vader was using Leia and Han
to trap Luke Skywalker.
Darth Vader knew Luke would
try to rescue his friends.

Darth Vader was right.
Luke had sensed that his friends
needed help.

Luke and his droid R2-D2
were flying to Cloud City!

Darth Vader was going to
freeze Luke in carbonite.
But Darth Vader decided to test
the machine and freeze Han first.

Then Boba Fett was going
to take Han to Jabba the Hutt.
Jabba the Hutt was a mean alien.
Han owed Jabba money.

Han said good-bye to
Leia and Chewie.
Then he was frozen.

Luke arrived to help his friends.
Leia tried to tell Luke
that it was a trap.
But the troopers carried Leia away.

Luke searched for his friends.
But he found Darth Vader instead.
Luke ignited his lightsaber.

Darth Vader ignited his lightsaber.
Luke and Darth Vader began to duel.

Meanwhile, Lando freed
Chewie and Leia.
Lando did not like Darth Vader.
Lando wanted to save Han!

Boba Fett was loading
Han onto his ship.
Lando, Chewie, and Leia
ran to the platform!

But they were too late.
Boba Fett's ship blasted
into the sky.

Leia, Lando, Chewie, and C-3PO needed to get back to the *Falcon*. R2-D2 arrived just in time to help them!

Stormtroopers tried
to stop the team!
But Leia, Lando, Chewie, C-3PO,
and R2-D2 flew away in the *Falcon*!

Luke and Darth Vader continued to fight!
Darth Vader wanted Luke to join
the dark side of the Force.
Luke refused.

But Darth Vader was too strong.
Darth Vader struck Luke.
Luke dropped his lightsaber.
Luke's lightsaber fell away.
Then Darth Vader told Luke
that he was Luke's father!

Luke was shocked!
He needed to get away
from Darth Vader.

Luke decided to follow
his lightsaber.
Luke fell away from Darth Vader.

Luke grabbed on to an antenna.
He was all alone.
Luke did not know what to do.

Leia sensed that Luke
needed her help.

The team flew back to Cloud City.
They rescued Luke and
jumped to lightspeed.

Luke knew he would face
Darth Vader again.
But now was not the time.
They had to get back to the rebels.

Together, the heroes would find a way to save Han and defeat the Empire!